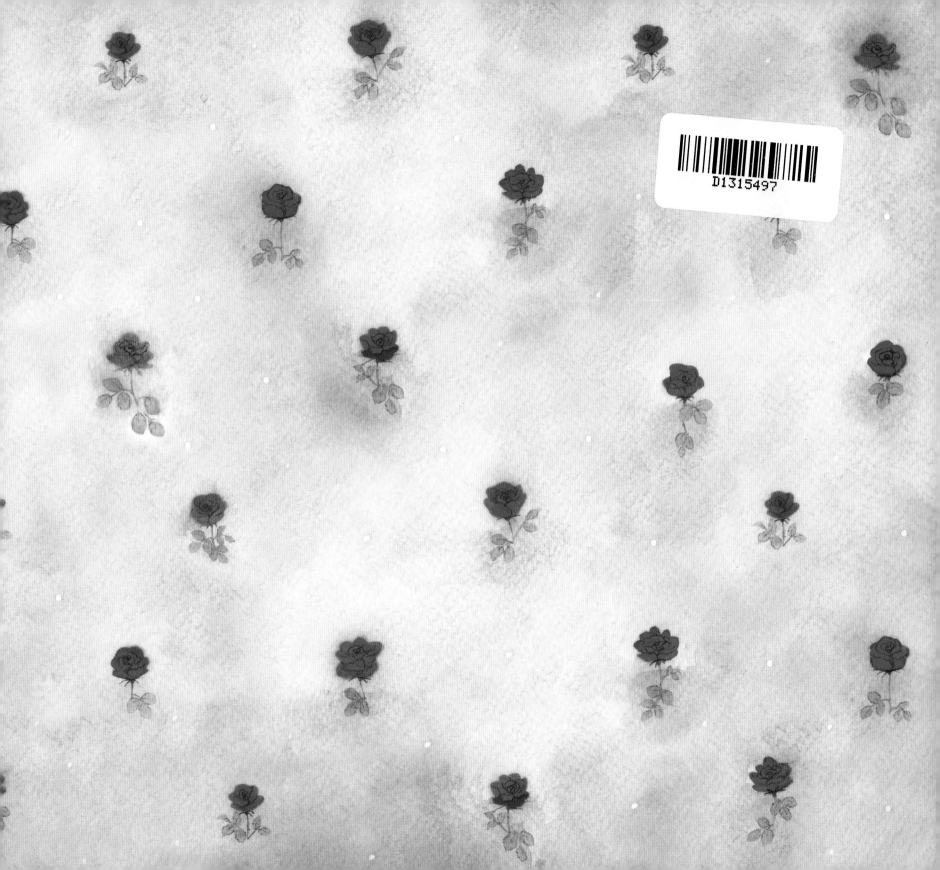

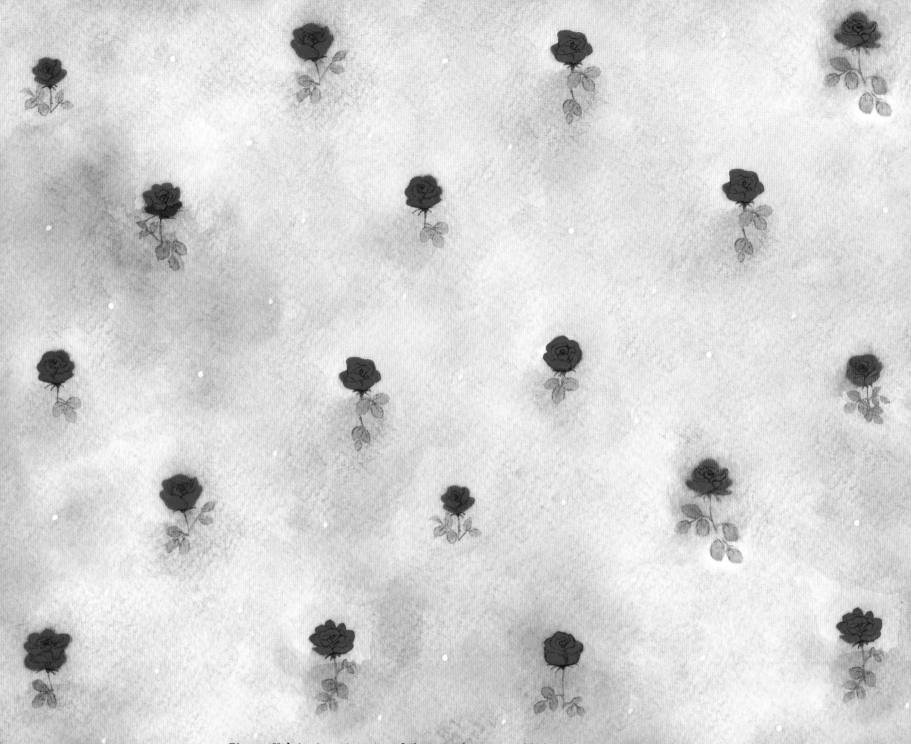

Picture Kelpies is an imprint of Floris Books. First published in 2016 by Floris Books
Text by Robert Burns. Illustrations © 2016 Ruchi Mhasane. Ruchi Mhasane asserts her right
under the Copyright, Designs and Patents Act 1988 to be recognised as the Illustrator of this Work
All rights reserved. No part of this book may be reproduced without prior permission of
Floris Books, Edinburgh www.florisbooks.co.uk The publisher acknowledges subsidy from Creative Scotland towards the
publication of this volume. British Library CIP Data available. ISBN 978-178250-322-4 Printed in China through Asia Pacific Offset Ltd

My Luve's Like a Red, Red Rose

To Amelia
with love from
Nanya +
Grandad
We thought of you
on our trip to
Scotland!
XO
June 2022

Words by Robert Burns
Illustrated by Ruchi Mhasane

Picture
Kelpies

O my Luve's like a red, red rose,
That's newly sprung in June;

O my Luve's like the melodie
That's sweetly play'd in tune.

As fair art thou, my bonnie lass,
So deep in luve am I;

And I will luve thee still, my dear,
Till a' the seas gang dry.

Till a' the seas gang dry, my dear,
And the rocks melt wi' the sun:

I will luve thee still, my dear,
While the sands o' life shall run.

And fare thee weel, my only Luve!
And fare thee weel, a while!

And I will come again, my Luve,
Tho' it were ten thousand mile!

Ruchi Mhasane was born in 1987 in India. Ruchi studied children's book illustration at Cambridge School of Art in England but she now lives where she grew up in the hot, bustling and colourful Indian city of Mumbai. It is very different from Burns' cold, quiet Scottish fields!

You may have heard of **Robert Burns**. He is probably the most famous Scottish writer *ever* and he wrote the words in this book. He was born on 25th January 1759 – that's over 250 years ago! He is *so* well known and loved that Scottish people celebrate his birthday every year by eating haggis, neeps and tatties (yum), and reading out his poems.

Robert Burns came from a small village called Alloway near Ayr in southern Scotland, where he worked as a farmer. He often made up rhymes while he was working outside in the fields. His most famous poems and songs include *To a Mouse, Tam o' Shanter* and *Auld Lang Syne*, which people all around the world sing at New Year. He even wrote a poem about a haggis!

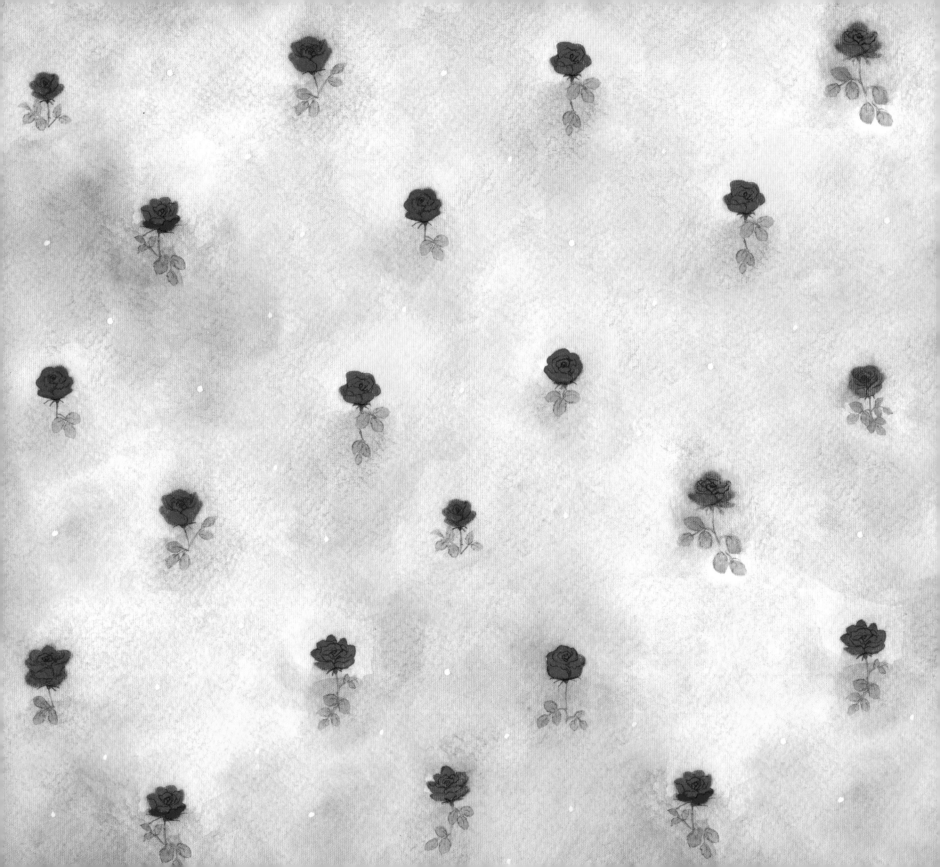